DETECTIVE
NOSEGOODE

and the
MUSIC BOX MYSTERY
Marian Orłoń

Illustrated by Jerzy Flisak

Translated by Eliza Marciniak

PUSHKIN CHILDREN'S BOOKS

Pushkin Press
71–75 Shelton Street
London, WC2H 9JQ

Original text © Maria Orłoń 2013
Illustrations © Piotr Flisak and Mikołaj Flisak 2013
English translation © Eliza Marciniak 2017

Detective Nosegoode and the Music Box Mystery was first published as *Ostatnia przygoda detektywa Noska* in 1968

First published by Pushkin Press in 2017

Published by arrangement of Wydawnictwo Dwie Siostry, Warsaw (Poland)

10 9 8 7 6 5 4 3 2 1

ISBN 13: 978 1 782691 55 6

Designed and typeset by Tetragon, London
Printed and bound by TJ International, Padstow, Cornwall

www.pushkinpress.com

AMBROSIUS NOSEGOODE, CODY AND BLACKBEARD

The clock on the tower struck six times, and Lower Limewood awoke from its slumber. The smell of fresh baking filled the air, milk churns jangled and vegetable carts rolled out onto the streets. Caretakers opened doors and set about their morning cleaning. Sleepy faces appeared in the windows. A new day had begun.

7

A few minutes after six o'clock, the inhabitants of a little house in Skylark Lane, Mr Ambrosius Nosegoode and his friend Cody, woke up as well.

Ambrosius was a retired detective, the author of an outstanding book called *How to Unmask a Thief* and, once upon a time, the bane of criminals everywhere. Now he was a considerate, kind-hearted elderly gentleman.

Indeed, it was hard to believe that this chubby figure could once have caused such panic in the criminal world. Or that his grey, balding head could once have solved the toughest of cases. Or that the name of Ambrosius Nosegoode had been well known not just in the big city where he had lived and worked, but far and wide beyond its borders. Yet it was all true. Those were wonderful times! Still, they were gone. Old age came, and Ambrosius felt the need for peace. He returned to his native Lower Limewood, bought a little house and settled in it with Cody. He spent his time relaxing, growing radishes and playing his flute in the evenings. He didn't in the least suspect that it would be here, in quiet Lower Limewood, that he would have another adventure.

Cody was a dog. He was an ordinary, shaggy mutt, but Ambrosius would never consider swapping him for another dog of a more noble breed, even if such a dog came with a gold collar studded with jewels. Cody, in addition to all his virtues (and a few minor flaws), possessed one extraordinary skill: he could converse with his master! He had learnt this art from Ambrosius, and it happened very naturally. Like many people who live alone, Ambrosius enjoyed talking to himself. Or rather, to himself and to his dog. He spoke about his adventures, about hard times and about a hundred other things. Cody listened. Listened and nothing more. Then, one day, when Ambrosius asked him how he was, Cody replied, as if it were the most natural thing in the world, "I'm very well, thank you, except the fleas are bothering me."

It's not hard to imagine what a shock Ambrosius must have experienced when he heard these words. He almost became ill. But after that, his conversations with his dog were no longer one-sided.

And now, this morning, Ambrosius had jumped out of bed first and was pulling on Cody's ear.

"Wakey-wakey, you sleepy head! Mrs Cracker's cockerel is hoarse from crowing and you still haven't budged. Time to wake up!"

Cody blinked a few times and yawned.

"I had a beautiful dream," he said sleepily. "I dreamt I was a butcher. I was standing behind the counter, surrounded by sausages, hams and bones... What a sight it was! The smells alone were making me dizzy... I was just about to take a bite out of the tastiest-looking ham when I heard your voice."

He yawned again and asked, "Ambrosius, don't dreams come true sometimes?"

Ambrosius looked thoughtful. "Yes, that's what I've been told. My aunt once dreamt that she had broken her leg. And imagine: the very next day, something did break. Only it wasn't anything of my aunt's, and it wasn't a leg – it was her neighbour's ladder. Even so, my aunt insisted that her dream had come true. Maybe yours will too."

"Maybe. But before it does, could you make us something to eat? That dream really gave me an appetite."

"In less than ten minutes, we'll have a breakfast fit for a king!"

"Well, all I need is one that's fit for a dog," Cody replied humbly.

After breakfast, the two friends started getting ready to go out. Every morning, they would walk together to the nearby newsagent's to buy newspapers. As usual, the detective picked up his small briefcase, which he always carried with him everywhere, called Cody over, and the two of them went out into the street.

Skylark Lane was undoubtedly the quietest street in Lower Limewood. Single-storey houses with green gardens lined the pavements and cats slept peacefully next to flowering geraniums in the windows.

But not in *all* windows. As they passed Mrs Hardtack's house, Cody pulled on Ambrosius's trouser leg and whispered, "Look in that window! Blackbeard is at his post!"

Ambrosius glanced discreetly to his right and noticed a silhouette behind the net curtain. He had no doubt that it was Blackbeard. He also had no doubt that a couple of watchful eyes were following him and Cody from behind the curtain.

The two friends had been intrigued by Blackbeard since the previous day. That's when the big sign that had been hanging on Mrs Hardtack's front gate – "Room for rent, full board and laundry services" – had been taken down, and a mysterious man with a bushy beard had moved in.

There would have been nothing extraordinary about this if it hadn't been for the fact that the stranger seemed excessively interested in Mr Nosegoode and his dog. Soon after his arrival, he had questioned Mrs Hardtack about them and then, over the course of the day, Ambrosius and Cody had bumped into him three times. It couldn't have been a coincidence. And here he was again...

"I'm liking this less and less," said Cody. "And anyway, my left ear has been itchy for the past three days, which is a sure sign that something unusual is going to happen. I'm convinced that there's a connection between this itch and that bearded man. Listen, maybe he's a criminal, someone you had sent to prison? Maybe he got out and now he's looking for revenge?"

"I don't think so. He doesn't look like a criminal to me."

"Doesn't look like a criminal? What do you mean?"

"Have you looked closely at his beard?" Ambrosius asked.

"Of course. It's black and thick."

"You haven't noticed anything else?"

"No."

"Then you've missed the most important thing: it's fake! And not only that: it's badly attached."

"Fake?" Cody repeated, surprised. He recovered a moment later. "You see! It's clear proof of his bad intentions. If he didn't have bad intentions, he wouldn't put on a fake beard."

"But maybe this beard is precisely what proves his innocence?" Ambrosius replied mysteriously.

"You can't mean that!" Cody said with indignation. "You're joking, aren't you?"

"I'm not joking. I'm completely serious."

Cody looked at his master doubtfully, as if to check that he really wasn't joking, and then decided to let it go. No, it was clear that they wouldn't see eye to eye on this matter. It was a good thing that he, Cody, didn't allow himself to be deceived by Blackbeard. After all, someone had to remain vigilant, he thought, as he felt the weight of responsibility settle on his shoulders.

Just at that moment, they reached the newsagent's stand and their conversation came to an end, since nobody except Ambrosius knew about Cody's ability to speak.

"Good morning, Mr Loop!" Mr Nosegoode greeted the newsagent. "Do you have anything for us today?"

"Of course, of course!" Mr Loop replied, passing Ambrosius the latest editions of *The Morning News* and *A Dog's Friend*, the two papers that the retired detective liked to read regularly.

Accompanied by his dog, Mr Nosegoode headed for a bench in the nearby square and opened the first newspaper. He started reading aloud in a lowered voice, since Cody was also interested in politics – not to mention the fact that he eagerly devoured all news from canine circles. But Cody couldn't concentrate on what was being read. His thoughts were occupied with Blackbeard.

THE MYSTERIOUS THEFT

Around the same time, the local clockmaker, Mr Ignatius Blossom, was heading down Barrel-Organ Street to his workshop. He was walking briskly, swinging his bamboo cane and enjoying the bright May morning. Apart from the weather, he had another reason to be pleased: the day before, he had managed to repair a very complicated old music box.

A few days earlier, Mr Swallowtail, the town chemist, had put the box on his counter and said, "I've come to see you with this little curiosity, even though I doubt you'll be able to fix it. This toy is almost a hundred years old and is fiendishly intricate, but I would be very obliged if you could repair it. It's a family keepsake, which has recently gained in importance for us. Would you be able to spend some time on it?"

Mr Blossom picked up the toy and examined it carefully. It was a small metal box with a porcelain dancer on top. Inside was a mechanism that played a melody and made the figurine spin round. Mr Blossom inspected the mechanism, poked at a few wheels, pressed a few springs and replied, "I think I can manage it. Please come back in a week."

And he did manage it. Admittedly, he spent many hours working on the toy, but not in vain. Only the previous afternoon, a lively melody had filled the workshop, and the dancer had turned gracefully. Mr Blossom had proved once again that he had a magic touch. So it was no wonder that he was in such a splendid mood that May morning.

The town-hall clock struck half past seven. Mr Blossom took out his thick pocket watch and with a glance determined – to his annoyance – that the clock on the tower was running two minutes early yet again. He didn't like unpunctual people or unpunctual clocks. *It will need to be adjusted*, he thought.

His workshop wasn't far now. At the sight of the familiar sign, "Ignatius Blossom, Clockmaker", with a large clock face above it, Mr Blossom quickened his pace. He climbed the little steps up to his workshop, took out his key and was about to put it in the lock, when all of a sudden he froze: the door was open! The first, utterly ridiculous thought that crossed his mind was that he had forgotten to lock it the night before. But at that very moment he noticed a fresh splinter sticking out of the wooden frame, and he understood: there had been a break-in!

For a few seconds, Mr Blossom stood petrified. Then, with a sense of foreboding, he pushed the door open and looked inside. He went no further for fear of destroying any clues that the burglar might have left behind.

The first thing he noticed was that the workshop was tidy. He had expected to see upturned furniture, open drawers, the large display case broken... But everything was in its place. The drawers were closed, pocket watches lay undisturbed under glass in the case, the large clocks on the wall ticked solemnly... Mr Blossom couldn't believe his eyes. Did the burglar not take anything?

He surveyed the room once again and only then noticed what was missing. "The music box..." he whispered. "The music box has been stolen!"

He stared in astonishment at the spot where the chemist's family keepsake had stood only the day before.

Is that really what the thief came for? he wondered to himself. *Why not something else? Why would somebody steal that specific music box but leave two gold watches behind?*

Mr Blossom couldn't think of answers to these questions. He stood on the threshold, helpless and worried, not sure what to do next. Of course, the easiest thing would be to report the theft to the police, but Mr Blossom didn't want the incident to attract a lot of attention. That could be damaging to the excellent reputation of his business.

What should I do? he kept asking himself, agitated. Then a bright idea came into his head. *Nosegoode! He's my great hope! He's the only one who can help!*

Mr Blossom quickly revived. In his mind's eye, he could already see the old detective leading the captured thief by the hand; he could see himself reclaiming the stolen music box. He was about to hurry off to get Mr Nosegoode when he realized that he couldn't leave the workshop unlocked.

"Oh, that Joey. He's late again..." he sighed.

Joey was Mr Blossom's apprentice. For the past three months he had been learning the difficult art of repairing clocks. Alas, he wasn't making much progress. Mr Blossom tried to explain this by the fact that Joey didn't have a heart for clocks. *You have to love clocks*, he'd say to himself. *A person who doesn't love clocks can never become a good clockmaker.*

On the other hand, Joey had a few flaws that genuinely worried Mr Blossom. First, as demonstrated that morning, he wasn't punctual and, according to Mr Blossom, an unpunctual clockmaker was as good as a tone-deaf organist. The master craftsman was trying to teach his pupil to be on time, but without much success.

Second, Joey had a habit of telling lies.

"Sir, could I be excused a little early this afternoon?" Joey had asked him one day. "My grandmother is ill, so I'd like to chop some wood for her and bring her fresh water..."

Moved by Joey's thoughtfulness, Mr Blossom had let him go without a moment's hesitation. Later on, he found out that Joey's grandmother had been at a wedding that day and that Joey had spent his free time fishing by the river with his friends.

Finally, Joey had once stolen something, and this upset the clockmaker most of all.

For all these reasons, Mr Blossom couldn't talk about his apprentice without feeling rather bitter.

Thinking of him now, he furrowed his brow. A suspicious thought crossed his mind, but he dismissed it straight away.

"Good morning, sir!" A cheerful voice broke into his thoughts. "I see you're not hurrying to start work this morning either! No wonder, such great weather..."

The clockmaker snapped out of his musings and looked at his apprentice. Joey had a long nose and a thick mop of impossibly red hair. He was gazing up at the master craftsman with a wide smile, but he grew serious as soon as he noticed the worried look on his face.

"Mr Blossom, has something bad happened?" Joey asked anxiously.

"I'm afraid it has," the clockmaker answered in a downcast voice. "A thief has broken into the workshop."

"A thief?! But that's impossible..."

"Unfortunately, it's very possible."

"Did the thief steal anything?"

"Yes. Thieves always steal things."

"So... what's missing, Mr Blossom?"

The clockmaker cast a quick but searching glance at Joey and said, "The chemist's music box."

"The music box?" Joey repeated, incredulous. "Why would a thief want a music box?"

"Well, that's a question you'd need to ask the thief!" Mr Blossom smiled sourly.

Joey tugged nervously at his unruly hair. He couldn't understand the thief's odd choice.

"Sir, this theft is very mysterious," he said at last. "Are you going to report it to the police?"

Mr Blossom looked at him carefully again.

"Not just now. First I'm going to talk to someone who can be of more help to us than the police. That's where I'm heading now. In the meantime, you're going to guard the workshop. Make sure you don't let anyone in, and don't go inside yourself. If anyone passes by, just pretend that nothing's happened and that you're simply waiting for me. You're going to do a good job, I hope?"

"Yes, sir, you can rest assured!" Joey promised. He was glad that the old master had given him such an important task.

Mr Blossom left Joey at his post and hurried off towards the square, where he hoped to find Mr Nosegoode. He knew the detective's habits and expected to see him sitting on a bench, flipping through the morning papers.

He wasn't disappointed.

Mr Nosegoode was just finishing reading the last page of *A Dog's Friend* when the clockmaker appeared.

"Mr Nosegoode!" Mr Blossom said breathlessly. "I need your help! I've been robbed!"

He recounted what had happened.

It was incredible just how much the old detective seemed to change as he listened to this short tale. He straightened up, his cheeks became flushed, his eyes lit up. It was as if a full ten years had fallen away from him. Cody also became strangely possessed. He wanted to shout, "Didn't I say that something unusual would happen?"

"Mr Nosegoode..." the clockmaker said, coming to the end of his story. "I have to get that music box back! You're my only hope! Please, say you will help."

Ambrosius got up from the bench.

"We'll catch the thief, I promise you!" he said decisively. "Now, let's go to your workshop."

The clockmaker breathed a sigh of relief. Feeling hopeful, he set off down Barrel-Organ Street with Mr Nosegoode and his dog.

MR NOSEGOODE BEGINS
TO INVESTIGATE

There was no doubt that Joey was doing a great job at his assigned post. He was standing casually in the doorway, staring at three sparrows hopping in the road. Nobody would have suspected that he was guarding a spot where a crime had been committed.

"And over there is Joey," Mr Blossom explained in a hushed voice when they got near.

"Hmm, an interesting boy," Mr Nosegoode declared, observing Joey carefully.

He had clearly been intrigued by Joey a few minutes earlier, when the clockmaker mentioned that he had an apprentice. The detective had even asked for a brief description of the boy's character. After hearing what Mr Blossom had to say, he posed an awkward question: "Has it occurred to you that Joey...? Well, you understand what I'm getting at."

Mr Blossom nodded and then hesitated.

"Yes," he admitted a moment later. "The thought did occur to me, but I've dismissed it. I don't think Joey would be capable of such a thing. It's true that he's no angel and that he's got his faults, but I don't think he could commit a theft like this. And anyway, why would he want to steal a music box? It has no value for him at all. He was very surprised when he learnt what had happened."

Mr Blossom pondered something in silence and then added, as if to convince himself, "No, it's not possible. Joey couldn't have done it."

"No, no, of course not," Mr Nosegoode agreed quickly.

They reached the front of the workshop and stopped. The arrival of the famous detective made quite an impression on Joey. Clearly, he hadn't expected the master clockmaker to ask such an illustrious figure for help. So, when this illustrious figure reached out his hand to shake Joey's, the boy blushed deeply.

"Have you noticed anything suspicious?" Mr Nosegoode asked him.

"No."

The detective cast a glance around them.

"We're very lucky that the street is deserted. Otherwise we'd soon have a crowd of onlookers on our hands, and that's something I'd rather avoid. I'm a bit worried about the woman in the window across the street, who is definitely paying far too much attention to our humble selves... But there is little to be done about it. We can put up with one spectator."

With these words, he opened his briefcase, pulled out a powerful magnifying glass and went up to the door. He looked at it briefly and said, "The thief wasn't very inventive. An ordinary crowbar was used to break the lock. The mark is very clear. But a crowbar mark is not enough. We must find other clues."

He lifted the magnifying glass up to his eyes again and began to examine the door carefully.

"Yes..." he muttered. "Yes, we must find other clues. Ah, here's one: a piece of thread! A black silk thread...

It's caught on a splinter made by the crowbar, so it must have been left behind by the thief. I already have an idea of where it might have come from. But, for now, let's put it in an envelope. Maybe this thread will lead us to a solution..."

Mr Nosegoode unhooked the thread carefully, placed it inside an envelope and went back to examining the door.

"I have reason to suspect that the thief didn't leave any fingerprints," he said. "Let's check if I'm correct. Mr Blossom, when was the last time this door was washed?"

"Joey washed it yesterday after we closed up," the clockmaker answered. "We do a thorough clean every Wednesday."

"Very good. This means that we should find only your fingerprints and Joey's, and possibly the thief's. We'll know in a minute if this is true."

The detective leant over his briefcase and took out a small box, a brush and a roll of tape. The box contained white powder, with which Ambrosius dusted the door in a few spots. He then swept these spots with the brush and examined them under the magnifying glass.

"I see only two kinds of fingerprints," he remarked. "I'm sure these are yours and your apprentice's, but it won't hurt to preserve them, just in case."

He pressed pieces of tape against the areas he had dusted, then peeled the tape away and put the pieces in another envelope. An exact image of the fingerprints was preserved on the tape.

"Now we can go inside," he announced. "I'll lead the way, if I may."

Mr Nosegoode stepped over the threshold, followed by Mr Blossom and Joey. Cody slipped in behind them, sat down by the wall and continued to follow everything diligently.

After casting his eyes all around the workshop, Ambrosius concentrated his attention on the floor. He must have noticed something interesting because he crouched down and gazed intently at one spot.

"Mr Blossom." He turned to the clockmaker. "Is this footprint yours?"

Mr Blossom crouched down next to the detective. He looked at the shoe print visible on the freshly polished floor and shook his head. "No, I don't own shoes like that."

"What about you, young man?"

Joey said it wasn't his footprint either.

"In that case, we can conclude that it must be the thief's. Let's copy it. It might come in handy."

Mr Nosegoode opened his notebook and sketched the pattern of the sole.

"And now," he said, closing his notebook, "could you tell me precisely where the stolen music box was standing yesterday?"

Mr Blossom pointed straight ahead. "It was over there, on that shelf."

"It's not a particularly noticeable spot," Mr Nosegoode remarked. Not taking his eyes off the floor, he walked over to the shelf. He stopped in front of it, swept it with his eyes and reached out his hand to grab something.

"Does this belong to you, Mr Blossom?" he asked.

In his open palm was a matchbox.

The clockmaker checked his pockets.

"No, my matches are right here."

Mr Nosegoode looked over at Joey.

"I... I don't carry matches at all. I... I don't smoke," replied the apprentice, visibly flustered.

"Well, this means the thief has left us another souvenir," said Ambrosius, pretending not to notice Joey's discomfort. "It's a valuable one, too," he added, examining something written on the box.

Nobody could observe what that something was because Mr Nosegoode quickly put the matchbox into his briefcase.

"We should be able to find more traces," he said. He looked around again and exclaimed, "Here's another!"

He bent over and picked up a spent match from the floor. He glanced back down.

"Only one?" He considered this for a moment. "Interesting, very interesting..."

The match followed the box into the briefcase.

Mr Nosegoode wandered around the workshop for a while, looking here and there, but he didn't find anything else. At last, he sat down in a chair and declared, "Now I'd like to ask both of you a few questions."

Mr Blossom and Joey also sat down. Cody pricked up his ears, and the old detective began the questioning.

"Can you please tell me if there was anyone else present when the chemist came in with the music box?"

"No," came a decisive answer.

"Did anyone else express any interest in it later?"

"Yes," the master and his apprentice answered at the same time.

Mr Nosegoode shifted anxiously.

"Who?" he asked.

"A man with a black beard," the clockmaker said. "A stranger, not from these parts. He came here yesterday and asked me to replace his watch glass. When I got down to work, he started looking around the shelves as if he

were in a museum, not in a clockmaker's workshop. Then I heard his voice: 'Excuse me, is this toy for sale?' I looked up and saw him pointing to the music box. 'No, it's not,' I answered. 'The owner dropped it off to be repaired.' To which he said, 'That's too bad. I'm interested in these kinds of things, and I like to buy them when I can.' That's what he said. Yesterday I didn't pay the least bit of attention to his words, but now... Do you think it's him?"

"It's far too early to think anything," the detective answered evasively.

Although this piece of information about Blackbeard did not appear to make a very strong impression on Mr Nosegoode, it had a huge effect on Cody. The dog was triumphant. He stretched out his tail proudly. Seeking Ambrosius's eyes, he seemed to be saying, "Well, you see, I was right! I wasn't deceived by that fake beard. I can't be deceived so easily!"

But Ambrosius wasn't paying any attention to Cody.

"Apart from this stranger, did anybody else seem interested in the music box?" he continued.

Mr Blossom scratched his forehead. "I don't think so..." he said, trying to remember. "I don't think so..."

"One last question: apart from you and Joey, who knew that the music box had been fixed yesterday?"

"Only the chemist."

"When did you tell him?"

"Yesterday afternoon. He sent his nephew to check on it. I told the boy that the music box was ready, and he was very glad to hear it. 'My uncle can hardly wait,' he said as he was leaving. But the chemist never came. If only he had come yesterday, this would never have happened... And now what? No doubt he'll come today. What am I going to say to him? That his music box has been stolen?"

"You don't need to worry," the detective said calmly. "I'm going to be talking to Mr Swallowtail very shortly, and I will inform him myself about the theft. I will also reassure him that he will soon have his music box back."

"Thank you so much."

Mr Nosegoode got up. Closing his briefcase, he continued, "It's only a matter of time before the thief is identified. The guilty person left far too many traces. All I'm missing is the key to this mystery. I'm hoping to find that key at the chemist's, which is where I'm going next."

He said goodbye and left the workshop with Cody.

Once they were out on the street, the dog burst out, "Really, Ambrosius! I don't understand you. What do you mean by 'It's only a matter of time before the thief is identified'? What is there to think about? We know who the thief is already."

"We do?"

"Of course. It's crystal clear who stole the music box."

"Is it now? Not to me."

"To me it is."

"I'm afraid your nose has let you down," Ambrosius replied.

"Don't you joke about my nose!" Cody said in an offended tone. "You know very well how useful it has proved in the past. And I do know who the thief is. In fact, you don't need a nose for that – you just need a head."

Ambrosius smiled indulgently.

"Oh, Cody, Cody... You're too hasty in your judgements. This case is not as simple as you seem to think. But I'd rather not talk about it until later. Especially since we have a good reason to be silent."

"What reason? I don't know what you're talking about."

"Look behind you!"

Cody glanced back – and shivers ran down his spine. Walking just a few steps behind them was... Blackbeard!

THE STORY OF
THE MUSIC BOX

The Pelican Pharmacy was located in an old townhouse. The decorative sign on the front of the building was shaded by centuries-old lime trees at the edge of the pavement. It was under one of these trees that Mr Nosegoode had stopped and, pretending to tie a shoelace, cast a glance behind him. The bearded man had also stopped.

"He's still tailing us," Ambrosius whispered.

"I'm not surprised," Cody muttered in reply, and both of them headed for the door to the pharmacy.

Mr Boniface Swallowtail was preparing gout ointment in a mortar when the bell on the front door tinkled.

"Welcome, Inspector!" he said brightly, straightening up from his work. "To what do I owe this pleasure? Not an illness, I hope?"

It was only now that the old detective realized his mission was not exactly a happy one. How was he to tell this nice, friendly man, who looked after his health and called him "Inspector", that he had such unpleasant news?

"We've come to see you about a rather troublesome matter," he began, searching for the right words.

Mr Swallowtail put away the mortar and pestle, adjusted his glasses and looked enquiringly at Mr Nosegoode. The detective's words had aroused his curiosity so much that he didn't even notice the bearded face pressed up against the shop window. It disappeared only a moment later, but not before the detective and his dog had noticed it; they stealthily exchanged a glance.

"Our visit has to do with your music box," the detective continued.

"My music box? I'm sorry, but how do you know about my music box?"

"From Mr Blossom."

The chemist furrowed his brow. He was beginning to guess the truth.

"Has... has something bad happened?" he asked anxiously.

Mr Nosegoode nodded.

"It's been stolen, hasn't it?"

"Yes, I'm afraid it has."

Mr Swallowtail's face fell.

"But who on earth could steal it?" he burst out. "Nobody outside my family knew that the..." He stopped, realizing he'd said too much.

"At the moment, I can't answer this question," the detective replied, "but I can reassure you that the one responsible will be caught. I'll do my best – but I need you to help me. I'm guessing there's a secret of some kind attached to the music box. I don't know what it is – but you do. The thief knew it too. Understanding this secret will be crucial..."

Mr Swallowtail took off his glasses and carefully wiped the lenses. He put the glasses back on, looked straight into Ambrosius's eyes and said, "I'm going to help you. I will tell you the secret, although it may seem ridiculous. I have to say I'm not sure what to think of it myself."

He gestured for Mr Nosegoode to make himself comfortable in one of the armchairs and came out from behind the counter to join him. Without waiting for an invitation, Cody curled up on the rug and pricked up his ears.

"The story I'm going to tell you," the chemist began, "goes back to the time of my grandfather. He too lived in this house, and he too was a chemist – and, according to family tales, a real oddball. He devoted the greater part of his life to searching for a miraculous cure which would bring him everlasting fame. He died, however, without achieving his goal. The last sign of his eccentricity was one little paragraph in his will, which caused a great stir among all the members of the family. It referred to some treasure which my grandfather had supposedly left to his descendants. 'Look for it yourselves,' he wrote. 'The one who follows my path will find it.'

"You can just imagine," the chemist continued, "what happened after the will was read out. They nearly turned the house upside down. But to no avail: they didn't find the treasure. The search was renewed many times afterwards, always with the same result. Ultimately, all the inheritors came to the conclusion that there had never been any treasure and that the old man had simply played a practical joke on the family. My father, who told me the whole story, shared this opinion. Years and years went by and the treasure was forgotten – until memories of those tales suddenly came flooding back. About a month ago, I was flipping through some old medical books which I had inherited from my grandfather, and in one of them I came across this note."

Mr Swallowtail reached into his pocket, pulled out his wallet, produced a yellowed piece of paper covered with handwriting and handed it to Mr Nosegoode. Ambrosius lifted it up to his eyes and – for Cody's benefit – read the contents out in a low voice: "'Hark, whoever you are! I have left a treasure, and I am now bequeathing it to you. Let it be a reward to you for reading these wise books. A dancing girl will show you the way to this treasure.'"

"So it's true after all!" Mr Nosegoode declared. He wanted to add something, but the chemist took up his story again.

"Yes, this note seemed to confirm that the mention of treasure in the will wasn't a joke," he continued. "But it also posed a new challenge: this 'dancing girl'. Who was this girl? Where could she be found? I'd probably still be trying to puzzle it out if it weren't for a coincidence. Last week, my daughter and I went up to the attic. We were looking for something among all the old junk, Jill

in one corner and me in another. Suddenly I heard her calling, 'Dad! Take a look at this beautiful dancer!' I got a funny feeling. I went over and saw Jill holding an old music box that had been kicking around the attic for years. When I took a look at it – when I saw the porcelain dancer on top – the 'dancing girl' ceased to be a mystery. I had her right in front of me. But soon a new problem presented itself: what to do to make the music box break its silence. Because no matter how hard I tried to wind it or tap at it, it was silent as if spellbound. I concluded that

the mechanism was broken and needed to be repaired. That same day, I took it to Mr Blossom, whose talent and diligence I greatly respect. You already know the rest."

The chemist fell silent and appeared lost in thought. His furrowed brow confirmed that what he was thinking about wasn't pleasant. And no wonder – great fortune had been within his grasp, but it had passed him by.

Mr Nosegoode was the first to break the silence.

"Your story," he said, "provides a key link in the chain of my investigations. I finally know the motive for the theft. I know why the thief stole a seemingly insignificant toy – but I still don't know who the thief is. That's why I need to ask you some more questions. Can you tell me who – apart from you – knew about the treasure, the note you had found and the music box?"

The chemist answered without hesitation.

"My whole family knew about them. That's to say, my wife, my daughter, my son and my nephew."

"You didn't mention it to anyone else by any chance?"

"No."

"But could someone have overheard your conversations?"

"Overheard our conversations?" The chemist paused. "Yes, I suppose so. We talked about it quite freely. Next to an open window, in the garden..."

"Then we can assume that any of your tenants could have known about the treasure," Mr Nosegoode said. "May I have their names?"

"The Broomes, the Butterleys, the Hummings—" Mr Swallowtail began listing them.

"The Hummings?" the detective interrupted him. "I think I've already heard this name somewhere today. I wonder where..."

"It must have been at the clockmaker's. Young Joey Humming is Mr Blossom's apprentice and..."

The chemist broke off and looked at the detective wide-eyed, as if he had unexpectedly made a great discovery.

Ambrosius pretended not to notice and replied casually, "You're right. That's where I heard it." And before Mr Swallowtail could say anything, he asked, "When were you planning to pick up the music box?"

The chemist was visibly disappointed by this change of topic.

"Today," he said. "Ben told me about half an hour ago that it was ready."

"Who's Ben?"

"My sister's son. He's been living with us for the past two weeks. He dropped out of school, had a quarrel with his father, and has now come to stay with his uncle."

Mr Nosegoode nodded sympathetically.

"Doesn't he miss home?"

"I think he does. He was going to go back for a visit today, but he slept in. He said he'll go the day after tomorrow."

"Right..." Mr Nosegoode said thoughtfully. "But let's get back to the music box! Is there anything else you can think of that might be connected to the theft?"

Mr Swallowtail spread out his arms helplessly.

"I think I've said everything..."

"You have indeed said a great deal," the detective acknowledged, rising from the armchair.

"A great deal?" Mr Swallowtail was surprised.

"Yes, I'm very grateful, and I expect that you'll have your music box back before long. See you soon!"

The chemist thanked Mr Nosegoode for taking on the case and accompanied his guests to the door. On the threshold, he stroked Cody's back, which confirmed the dog's conviction that Mr Swallowtail was a very nice person indeed.

Out on the street, life continued as usual. There were birds singing high up in a lime tree, a young woman was pushing a pram, and on the corner the postman was looking for something in his bulging bag. But the detective and his dog were not taking much notice of these things: all their attention was focused on the bearded man looking at books in a shop window. They exchanged meaningful glances and wordlessly headed towards home. A moment later, Blackbeard followed.

A TOUGH BONE
TO CRACK

An hour later, Ambrosius Nosegoode and his dog were sitting in their garden in Skylark Lane having an animated conversation. They were discussing the extraordinary events that had taken place that morning.

"My great friend detective Hippolytus Whiskers," Mr Nosegoode was saying, "had a golden rule that he always followed in his work. It went something like this: if we don't know what we want to know, let's reflect on what we do know, and that will lead us to what we don't know."

"I'm sorry," Cody interrupted him. "Could you repeat that?"

Ambrosius repeated what he'd just said.

"Thank you," the dog replied. "I think I've got it now."

Ambrosius nodded happily and continued.

"Let's apply this golden rule and try to list everything we know about the theft. To begin with, I would say that the theft itself is an indisputable fact."

"This discovery does you credit," Cody remarked.

Ambrosius thanked him with another quick nod.

"There is also no doubt," he resumed, "that the music box was stolen by someone who knew its secret. That's to say, someone who knew that it would lead to the treasure. Agreed?"

"No," the dog contradicted him. "The thief might not have heard about the treasure at all. He might have been a collector of mechanical musical instruments, for instance – someone who decided to steal this box only after he was told that it wasn't for sale."

"That's not impossible," Ambrosius admitted, "but I'm not convinced. I don't think a collector would have committed a break-in. It's too risky. Besides, they tend to be refined, cultured people, and somehow I just can't imagine a collector in the role of a burglar."

Cody waved the suggestion aside with his tail.

"Fine. If you don't want to believe that Blackbeard might be the thief, then suit yourself! I know a few people who didn't trust their dogs, and things didn't turn out too well for them."

"How curious!" the detective retorted. "Because I know a few dogs who didn't trust people, and things didn't turn out too well for them either. But never mind... Let's get back to Hippolytus Whiskers's golden rule. My theory is supported by the fact that the music box disappeared straight after being repaired. It would seem that it wasn't worth anything to the thief while it was broken."

"That could have been a coincidence," Cody muttered.

"It could have been, but it didn't *have* to be," the detective pointed out. "In general, there are fewer coincidences in life than we imagine."

"So whom do you suspect of the theft?" asked Cody, clearly impatient with Ambrosius's deliberations.

"One of the people who knew the secret of the music box, who was aware that the box had been repaired and who was also very familiar with the inside of the workshop. You're wondering why I think that the thief knew the workshop well? I learnt this from the match I discovered there. A single match! If the thief hadn't been familiar with the workshop, one match wouldn't have given them enough time to find the music box. It was night after all."

"I don't know whom you have in mind," Cody said, "but if you're excluding Blackbeard from your list of suspects, you're making a mistake. Can't you see that all the signs point to him? The bearded man visits the clockmaker, he sees the music box and wants to buy it, he's informed that it can't be sold, he's disappointed – and then the music box disappears overnight... Is there any reason for doubt here? Can you truly suspect anyone else?"

He fell silent and watched the impression his words made on Ambrosius. But the detective shook his head.

"You may be right," he said, "but there are more suspects than that. Take Joey Humming, for instance. One can make quite a convincing case against him. Listen to this. Joey lives in the same house as the chemist. He accidentally overhears a conversation about the treasure and learns that a music box is the key to finding it. This is the same music box that's at Mr Blossom's workshop. What could be simpler than to walk off with it and claim the treasure for himself? So Joey bides his time until the master manages to fix the box and then steals it. No doubt you're going to say that this is all just speculation. Agreed! But there are certain facts that are clearly against Joey. Did you notice his behaviour? Did you see how he went bright red when I arrived at the workshop? How uncomfortable he looked when I asked him about the matches? And there's one more thing: Joey has taken other people's property before. That has to be kept in mind.

So what do you think? Are you still sure that Blackbeard is our only suspect?"

Cody scratched his head uneasily.

"You've given me a tough bone to crack," he confessed.

"Bones are your speciality," the detective said, smiling.

Cody wrinkled his nose and batted away a fly buzzing around his ear. He was thinking.

"I've got it!" he cried out, struck by a sudden thought. "Joey didn't do it!"

"Why not?"

"If Joey had wanted to steal the music box, he wouldn't have had to break the lock. He could have just copied the keys. He had easy access to them."

Mr Nosegoode looked at his dog with genuine admiration, but he had to disappoint him again.

"Perhaps he didn't have time," he replied. "Or he didn't want to copy them..."

"Didn't want to? Why wouldn't he want to?"

"Because it would look suspicious."

Cody didn't know what to say in response. Feeling helpless, he let his tail drop.

"In that case, here's another question. If there are so many suspects, how are you going to prove who the thief is?"

"Well, I have reasons to focus on one of the suspects more than the others," Ambrosius replied. "I have paid special attention to this person... and I'm hoping to find the proof right here!"

Ambrosius slipped his hand into his jacket pocket, pulled out the matchbox the thief had left behind in Mr Blossom's workshop and put it under Cody's nose.

"Fingerprints?" the dog said, brightening up.

"Sadly, no. The thief was wearing gloves."

"Gloves? How do you know?"

"From the black silk thread that I found on the door of the workshop. This kind of thread could only have come from a glove – from a woman's glove, in fact!"

"Does this mean that the thief is a woman?"

"I didn't say that. Now take a look at these numbers."

It was only now that Cody noticed the column of numbers written on the box in ink. It read as follows:

4.25

7.15

21.30

"It looks as though the thief was noting down expenses," the dog remarked.

"Well done!" the detective said with approval. "I thought so too at first. But then another idea came to me."

"What was that?"

"I'll tell you tomorrow. Tomorrow I'm planning to do a little tour of Lower Limewood, which should clear up a few things in my mind. It's true I could do it today, but I don't like too much excitement all at once. We've had enough for now."

"And what if you don't manage to decode those numbers? What then?"

"We'll turn our attention to the other souvenirs which the thief has left behind. They might prove invaluable. Don't worry, my friend! The thief will not get away with it!"

Cody grew thoughtful. Much of what Ambrosius had said was unclear. Cody didn't understand all of it, but he was starting to believe that Ambrosius really would catch the thief. He was even prepared to admit that it might not be Blackbeard.

Mr Nosegoode's voice interrupted his thoughts.

"And now let's refresh our minds a little!" the detective exclaimed merrily. "Nothing reinvigorates the mind and restores mental balance like a bit of weeding in the radish patch. Let's get to work!"

A few minutes later, Ambrosius and his dog were engaged in a fierce battle with weeds. The detective was pulling them out with his hands, while the dog was using his teeth. It was hard to say which of them was better at this task. Busy with work, they forgot for a while about the treasure, the music box and the thief.

In fact, they probably wouldn't have returned to the subject until the following day, had it not been for Mrs Hardtack's visit that evening.

The two friends were heartily enjoying their supper of scrambled eggs with fresh chives when their neighbour appeared at the window.

"I just wanted to pop by to tell you," she said, out of breath, "that the bearded man was asking about you again,

Mr Nosegoode. About you and Cody. He wanted to know if you sleep in the same room or separately. I have no idea what to think any more! I hope nothing bad happens!"

"Not to worry, Mrs Hardtack," the detective said gently. "Nothing bad is going to happen. Curiosity is natural – and why not satisfy it. Please tell your tenant that we sleep

in one room and that we dream happy dreams. I'm sure he'll be pleased."

Mrs Hardtack muttered something under her breath and hurried off home. It was impossible to tell whether these words had put her mind at rest or made her even more agitated. What was perfectly clear, however, was that her visit had really rattled Cody. It rekindled all his suspicions about Blackbeard. The worst scenarios were crowding in his head.

"Ambrosius!" he burst out after the initial shock had worn off a bit. "I almost let you convince me that Blackbeard was innocent! It's lucky I've come to my senses before it's too late. He's a dangerous man, believe me! I'm sure he stole the music box and... and he's capable of anything!"

These last words sounded ominous but Ambrosius took them calmly. Cody was getting desperate. *How can I convince him?* he wondered.

"I'll find proof that Blackbeard is guilty," he said with sudden resolution. "Just give me a free hand tomorrow – or free paw, rather – to investigate. I'll follow his every move and unmask him!"

Ambrosius was moved by the passion with which Cody had spoken.

"I'm giving you a free paw to investigate tomorrow," he said solemnly.

That night, Cody hardly slept a wink. He was watching over his friend and thinking about the following day. He finally dozed off at dawn, when the stars disappeared from the sky and the birds began singing in the lilacs outside.

MR NOSEGOODE
BEHAVES STRANGELY

Mr Nosegoode finished shaving. He put the cut-throat razor aside and examined his face in the mirror, noting the white traces of soap. He ran his fingers down his chin and, without taking his eyes off his reflection, asked Cody, "What time are you setting off?"

"Same time as you. Immediately after breakfast.

You'll go off on your errands, and I'll wait for Blackbeard at the front. As soon as I see him, I'll start tracking him. I'll watch his every move."

"You really expect to find proof that the owner of that fake beard is a criminal?"

"I do. If I didn't expect it, I wouldn't traipse after him all over town. I'd lie in the garden, warming my old bones in the sun."

Ambrosius rinsed his face, wiped it with a towel and reached for his aftershave.

"Are you sure you won't choose the garden after all?"

Cody gave him an indignant look.

"How can you say that? You know that I don't break my resolutions."

"Unfortunately, I do know!" the detective sighed.

"What do you mean, 'unfortunately'? Maybe you don't think a dog should keep his resolutions?"

"Not at all!" Ambrosius protested and began preparing breakfast.

For a little while, Cody pretended to be offended, but when milk, cottage cheese and fresh buns appeared on the table, there was no trace of resentment remaining.

At eight o'clock, the two friends left the house. A bright morning greeted them outside. The sky was cloudless, and the garden resounded with birdsong. Ambrosius inhaled the brisk air and asked his dog, "Where are you going to wait for Blackbeard?"

Cody looked around for a hiding place. "Behind that wild rose bush. There's a good view of Mrs Hardtack's house from there."

Ambrosius complimented him on his choice and then gave him a gentle flick on the nose.

"Well, take care!" he said.

Cody suddenly realized that he'd soon be alone, without his friend, left to his own devices. For a moment, his resolve wavered. *Maybe I should back out?* he thought. *Maybe I should tuck in my tail and let Blackbeard be? Why risk an encounter with a criminal?* But his hesitation didn't last long. No, he wouldn't abandon his plan. He would prove to Ambrosius that the owner of the black beard wasn't an innocent collector of music boxes. He'd open his eyes to the danger. He had to do it!

Ambrosius was already by the gate. He was struggling with the latch.

"Ambrosius!" the dog called wistfully. "If something happens to me, remember that I've always..."

The detective waved goodbye.

"Tail up! Nothing's going to happen to you."

Cody didn't reply. He took cover behind the rose bush and from his hiding place watched his friend get further and further away.

*

Mr Nosegoode walks at an unhurried pace, strolling towards the newsagent's stand, as he does every morning. Passing Mrs Hardtack's house, he glances casually at the window, but there's nobody there. The net curtain doesn't budge. Mr Nosegoode starts whistling to himself.

He slowly approaches the news-stand. He stops in front of it, asks for his daily batch of newspapers, pays for them and continues on his way. He walks through the square, says hello to the baker and turns into Barrel-Organ Street. It looks as though he's going to visit Mr Blossom.

It's not far to the workshop now. But what's this? Mr Nosegoode suddenly crosses the street and quickens his steps. Evidently, he wants to avoid meeting the clock-maker. So where is he going? If he turns left, it means he's heading towards the train station; if he turns right, it's towards the chemist's.

He turns right. That means he must have something to discuss with Mr Swallowtail. But that's not it either – he slows down again, looking all around him. There is a clump of bushes, some newspapers strewn on the ground, a few empty beer bottles... Mr Nosegoode goes over to the bushes, leans down and pulls something out from under a branch. A pair of black silk gloves!

He lifts the gloves up to examine the initials embroidered on them before putting them in his pocket and continuing to look around the bushes. He's found something else! It's a length of iron bar. He inspects it and removes a sliver of wood from its end. He puts the splinter in a little box and wraps the bar in a newspaper. Now he's probably going to head for the pharmacy. But no. He's backtracking to the intersection and going to the train station.

A locomotive is puffing on the track, pigeons are cooing on the roof and a coachman is dozing in his horse-drawn carriage at the entrance to the station.

Mr Nosegoode takes it all in at a glance and goes up to the timetable posted on a board. He studies it with great interest. Seconds pass: one, two, three... There it is! It's clear from the detective's expression that he has found what he was looking for.

Unable to contain himself, he mutters, "It all adds up. I was right!"

These words attract the curiosity of the young woman at the ticket office, who raises her head from her paperwork to give Mr Nosegoode a concerned look.

Mr Nosegoode also startles the coachman when he rouses him out of his nap by asking to be driven to Barrel-Organ Street.

"Inspector! At this hour? Without any luggage? What a nice surprise! Would you like a blanket for your legs? No? Gee-up, lad, let's go!"

The horse's hooves clip-clop on the cobblestones and the carriage jolts up and down. Mr Nosegoode smiles to himself, while the coachman clicks his tongue at the horse. A turn to the right and they're in Barrel-Organ Street.

"Where would you like me to stop?"

"Two houses before the clockmaker's shop."

Two houses before the clockmaker's? How interesting! The carriage continues for a few dozen yards before coming to a halt. Mr Nosegoode hands some money to the coachman, jumps out onto the pavement and continues on foot towards Mr Blossom's workshop.

He goes up the steps and looks through the window. Only Joey is bustling about inside. Looking pleased, Mr Nosegoode goes in.

"Oh, hello, Inspector!" Joey cries out, blushing. "Have you caught the thief yet?"

"Almost," Mr Nosegoode answers. "Is the master in?"

"No, I'm afraid he's gone out. He went to fix the solicitor's clock. A tall, free-standing one. He'll be back in an hour."

"That's too bad," Mr Nosegoode says, but there is no trace of dismay on his face.

Joey wants to ask him all sorts of questions, but the detective doesn't give him time to speak. He begins asking questions himself.

"How is your aunt in Duckfield?" he enquires strangely.

Joey's eyes widen.

"My aunt in Duckfield? But I... I don't have an aunt in Duckfield!"

"Oh, no matter!" Mr Nosegoode laughs. "Perhaps an uncle of yours lives there? Or your brother-in-law?"

"I don't know anyone there!"

The detective doesn't stop smiling.

"And yet you're planning a trip to Duckfield," he says.

Joey's eyes widen even more.

"Me? To Duckfield? You've got it wrong, Inspector."

Mr Nosegoode pats him on the shoulder and says in a soothing tone, "You're right, I'm wrong. But I highly recommend a visit to Duckfield one day. It's a lovely town!"

Ambrosius goes out of the workshop, leaving Joey speechless. He walks back to Skylark Lane and doesn't stop until he reaches his house. Opening the gate, he calls out, "Cody! Cody!"

But Cody isn't there.

CODY IN DANGER

Cody wasn't there because he was following Blackbeard.

He didn't have to wait for him for long. At a quarter past eight, the gate in front of Mrs Hardtack's house creaked, and the owner of the fake beard appeared. Cody tensed his muscles. He realized that a risky game was about to begin – a game whose outcome he couldn't predict.

Blackbeard closed the gate carefully behind him, glanced in the direction of Mr Nosegoode's house, stroked his beard (*How strange that it doesn't fall off!* the dog thought) and set off towards the town centre. Cody waited a little while and then followed.

He didn't have an easy task. Blackbeard was behaving like a man who had plenty of time on his hands and wasn't in a hurry to get anywhere. He walked slowly, stopping for no reason and looking at whatever caught his eye. Every few steps, Cody had to jump off to the side to avoid attracting his attention. In this way, overcoming various obstacles, he reached the main square.

That's where the real trouble started. There was a market that morning, and the square was bustling with people. Traders were touting their wares, horses were neighing, geese were honking and a colourful, rowdy crowd filled every space. How could he track anyone in these circumstances? Blackbeard, meanwhile, was clearly taken with the place. He wandered from one stall to another without any apparent intention of leaving.

There really was a lot to see and hear!

One man, thin as a stick, was yelling in a hoarse voice, "Step up, ladies and gentlemen, step up! This is the only place where you can get the sensational Sparkle & Shine detergent. It can clean anything – absolutely anything, even stains on your honour! This amazing product, which I'm pleased to offer for a very low price, is world famous and one hundred per cent guaranteed! No need to push, there's enough for everyone. Here you go, ma'am! Who's next?"

Another seller, a chubby fellow, was loudly proclaiming the merits of combs made by Pranks & Company.

"Even old King Arthur himself used to groom his beard with a comb from Pranks!" he bellowed. "And today everyone uses our combs, ladies and gentlemen, because Pranks & Company combs are a mark of rare elegance

and true refinement! How many? Two? Here you go. We have a special offer: buy five and get a hairnet for free! Five for you, miss? Right away!"

To the left, someone was touting shoelaces, to the right – fattened geese; there were 'golden' rings over here and pots for cooking eggs over there. Somewhere not too far from Cody a barrel-organ whined and a parrot shrieked at the top of its voice.

Cody also caught other bits of information which were far more interesting. As he walked past two jolly women selling spring vegetables, he overheard a snippet of their conversation.

"Oh yes!" the first one said. "They stole a chest full of gold, my dear. They went in, carried it off and that was that. Now the clockmaker is tearing his hair out. He's lost a fortune..."

"But is that really true?" the other said doubtfully.

"What? You don't believe me?" the first bristled. "If you must know, Mrs Prune's cousin's sister-in-law, who's the clockmaker's neighbour, saw it with her own eyes!"

"A chest full of gold! Well, well," the other murmured.

Cody wasn't too surprised by this conversation – he knew a thing or two about humans' tendency to gossip – but he had to run when he realized he had lost sight of

Blackbeard. He had no trouble finding him in front of a rotund advertising pillar at the edge of the square.

Blackbeard was reading a huge poster, the contents of which had sent shivers down the spines of even the bravest dogs in Lower Limewood:

> Attention dog owners! By the mayor's order, a general vaccination of dogs against rabies will take place on Friday, 15th May. The vaccines will be administered in Billygoat Square by veterinarian Aloysius Pretzel. All dogs requiring vaccination must be brought washed and muzzled. Anyone found guilty of disobeying this order will be subject to imprisonment for up to seven days.

After reading this announcement and a few others, Blackbeard turned into Brewery Street, which was famous for its historic well. It was here that, according to old chronicles, the victorious King John Sobieski had stopped on his way back from the Battle of Vienna to let his horse drink. It was towards this well that Mrs Hardtack's tenant directed his steps.

What strange interests this man has, Cody thought. *One day it's music boxes, the next it's mildewy old wells. I wonder what he'll come up with tomorrow.*

Blackbeard examined the well's stonework roof, which was blackened with age, and read the plaque commemorating the king's momentous visit three centuries earlier. He scribbled something down in his notebook and, pulling at his beard, seemed to ponder what to do next. His decision was helped by the promising sign above a café across the street: "Sweet Corner".

Cody didn't like this café. He couldn't forgive the owner for the smaller sign on the door, which was an insult to dogs everywhere: "Please come in but leave your dog outside." *Dogs are not allowed, but the likes of him can enter no problem!* Cody thought bitterly when the door closed behind the bearded man.

He sat down on the edge of the pavement and reflected. He was disappointed. His hour-long pursuit of Blackbeard had not produced the results he'd expected. The man was behaving perfectly normally: no suspicious deeds, meetings or conversations. Just an ordinary tourist who happened to have a beard. Was Ambrosius right about him?

Cody didn't like to admit defeat. He tried to find some kind of explanation, some way to prove that he was right. And then it suddenly struck him.

I'm a donkey, not a dog! he told himself. *It's obvious why Blackbeard is behaving so innocently! He knows I'm following him. He knows I'm watching his every move – he must have seen me. He's probably gone into the café to try to lose me! I bet he's sitting by the window, sipping his coffee, pretending to read a newspaper, when in fact he's keeping an eye on me. Well, just you wait! We'll see who's going to outfox whom!*

Cody thought for a moment and quickly decided on his next steps. *I know what I'm going to do!* he thought. *I'll pretend I'm going home. He'll let his guard down, and then I'll hide somewhere and wait. When he leaves the café, I'll follow him, but I'll be more careful this time. I won't let him see me.*

He rose. Sluggishly, as befitted an old dog, he began dragging his paws homeward. When he was at a safe distance from the café, he regained his usual vigour, took a leap off to the side, crawled through a hole in a fence and hid in a garden. Finding a convenient observation spot, he decided to wait.

He waited a long time – an hour or more. He was beginning to suspect that Blackbeard had left by a hidden exit somewhere at the back of the café, when he finally saw him standing in front of Sweet Corner. *At last!* He breathed a sigh of relief and got up onto all fours.

The bearded man was still in no hurry. He paused. He looked left, then right, and after a brief hesitation started in the same direction as Cody. *Could he be going home?* the dog thought, worried. He waited to see what would happen next.

Blackbeard passed him, walked all the way to the square and disappeared in the crowd. Cody had been waiting for that: he sprang out of his hiding place and hurried after him. After cautiously looking around the square, he realized that Blackbeard was gone. He checked one street and then another. Only at the bottom of the third street, off in the distance, did he see the familiar silhouette of Blackbeard approaching Skylark Lane. Cody followed, quietly sneaking up behind him.

The closer he got, the more his mood fell. He hung his tail. It seemed he had been barking up the wrong tree: Blackbeard was going home. This meant that Cody's whole expedition had been in vain. He'd go back empty-pawed – and, what was worse, Ambrosius might think he'd been foolish.

When Blackbeard turned into Skylark Lane, Cody hung his tail even lower. The matter was settled. The last glimmer of hope had been extinguished. Tough. Perhaps he'd have better luck the following day.

*

Cody watches Blackbeard approach Mrs Hardtack's house. The man is already at the gate. He struggles with it for a moment, then opens it and disappears behind a clump of lilacs. Cody begins to drag himself home, hanging his head close to the ground. He stops thinking about the man and tries to imagine his meeting with Ambrosius. He's a step away from Mrs Hardtack's gate when suddenly he stops dead in his tracks: the gate swings open and... right there, standing in front of Cody, is Blackbeard!

"What a surprise!" the bearded man exclaims. "Such an interesting dog right in front of my house!" He lowers his voice. "I have a proposal for you, doggy. But let's talk about it over some milk, shall we? It would be my pleasure. Please come in!"

Cody remains rooted to the spot. *Is it a coincidence or a trick? Is he a friend or an enemy?* he asks himself. *What to do: accept his offer or make a run for it?*

"Come on, do come in!"

The man's voice sounds pleasant enough and his eyes seem friendly – but Cody knows that appearances can be deceiving.

If the worse comes to the worst, I can always escape in time, he thinks and steps inside.

The hallway is empty, as is the kitchen: Mrs Hardtack must have gone out shopping. This means they're alone. Cody hears the key being turned in the lock behind him. He lowers his tail all the way to the ground. He's completely at the mercy of the stranger.

Blackbeard leads Cody to his room. There's nothing suspicious inside: a suitcase, an umbrella, a big camera on a tripod, with the lens pointing at Cody. One glance at the table, however, and Cody's legs nearly buckle under him. There is a bottle of milk all right, but next to it is another, smaller bottle – labelled with a skull and crossbones.

Poison! Run! I have to get away! flashes through his mind.

Get away: but how? The window is closed; the key in the lock has been turned.

Blackbeard comes back from the kitchen holding a saucer. He goes up to the table.

Cody hears the splash of milk being poured out, but he can't see it – Blackbeard is blocking the view with his body. He's fiddling with something. It's not hard to guess: he must be opening the second bottle.

"Your treat is ready. Come and have some!" Blackbeard says. He picks up the saucer, carries it out into the hallway and puts it down in a corner.

"Don't be offended that it's not in my room, but I don't want to get in trouble," he explains. "Mrs Hardtack is very keen on cleanliness." He turns to Cody and continues, "Tasty cold milk! I think you'll like it."

Cody begins walking slowly towards this tasty cold milk. He knows he won't touch it, but he forces himself forward. At the same time, he's racking his brains to work out how to avoid being poisoned.

He bends over the saucer and pretends to drink. The man smiles encouragingly and goes back to his room.

"I just have to get something else ready," he says before closing the door behind him.

Cody seizes his chance. He's saved! He's surprised by how quickly an opportunity has come.

Yet far more surprised is Blackbeard when he hears a sharp, loud cry: "Open up! Police!" He rushes into the hall, turns the key in the lock and opens the front door.

That's exactly what Cody has been waiting for. One leap and he's free!

Without glancing back, he sprints towards home. How wonderful the air smells! How many birds there are in the trees! How warm the sun is! How far, far behind is that dreadful bottle with a skull and crossbones on it!

He's home already!

*

Cody stopped in front of the door with his tongue hanging out. His panting was so loud that only a moment later the door swung open and Ambrosius appeared.

"What happened, Cody?" the detective asked.

"Blackbeard has been exposed!" the dog gasped. "I was right, Ambrosius! He's a criminal! A poisoner!"

"A poisoner? What are you talking about?"

"A poisoner, one hundred per cent! He tried to poison me just now!"

Cody briefly explained what had happened.

"If he was trying to poison me," he concluded, "that means he must have a few things on his conscience. He'd noticed that I was trailing him and he wanted to get rid of me. Ambrosius! I swear on my nose that he's the one who stole the music box!"

Cody's story didn't seem to shock Ambrosius. On the contrary, he listened to it with a slight smile.

"Despite my great respect for your nose," he said after Cody had finished, "I can't agree with you. Blackbeard didn't steal the music box. It was someone else."

Cody was so astonished he had to sit down.

"Who?"

"It's a secret for now. But come inside and have a rest. There are still many adventures to come today."

As Cody plodded doggedly after Ambrosius, bitter thoughts attacked him like a swarm of hungry fleas.

That's human friendship and human gratitude for you! he thought. *I took on a dangerous mission, I nearly paid for it with my life, I got irrefutable proof that Blackbeard is a criminal – and what do I get? A little disbelieving smirk and a brand new secret, that's all. No hint of sympathy, no recognition of any kind. Was it worth the sacrifice?*

He didn't have time to answer his own question because just then the doorbell rang. It rang and it rang again, insistently.

"Who could it be?" Cody wondered out loud as his legs almost buckled under him once more.

Ambrosius didn't reply. With quick steps, he went up to the door and opened it.

Standing in the doorway was... Blackbeard!

WHO IS BLACKBEARD?

The bearded man looked as though he had just seen a visitor from another planet or a calf with two heads. He was completely flabbergasted.

"Please forgive me for this surprise visit," he said, wiping his forehead with a chequered handkerchief, "but a few minutes ago something so mysterious happened that I just can't explain it, which is why I've come to you for help."

"To me?" said Ambrosius, surprised.

"Yes. Because this mysterious incident involves your dog."

Cody quickly closed his eyes. Mr Nosegoode looked at him sternly, as if he wanted to scold him for being involved in mysterious incidents, and invited the guest in. He offered him an armchair, pulled a bottle of currant wine out of the dresser, filled the glasses and then said, "Now we can talk. Please tell me."

Blackbeard took a sip of his wine, glanced over at Cody – who was doing his best to keep calm – and began his story.

"Allow me first to introduce myself. My name is Timothy Pipestem. I'm a cynologist – a specialist in the study of dogs. Dogs are my life's passion. For the past few years, I've been working on a book titled *Portraits of Extraordinary Dogs*. I go from town to town and from village to village looking for interesting specimens. I record their habits; I take photographs. I came to your town a few days ago and met a few rather uninteresting dogs, but soon I came across yours. There's something about him that really intrigues me. It's hard to pin down. Maybe it's the exceptional intelligence you can see in his face; maybe it's the philosophical expression in his eyes.

I don't know. In any case, that's what made me follow you – you and Cody. I wanted to find out more about this ordinary-looking but in fact highly unusual mutt. Of course, I could've come to you, taken a closer look at him and asked you for the information I was after. But I decided to leave that for later. First I wanted to observe him in his natural environment, so to speak. I have to say my efforts paid off. Over the course of the next two days, I made a series of very interesting observations. I also obtained a few valuable details from Mrs Hardtack. All that was left was to take a few photographs." Blackbeard paused briefly.

"Well, a perfect opportunity presented itself about a quarter of an hour ago," he continued. "Your dog was right in front of my house. He was alone. I decided to invite him to my room so that I could take the photographs. He turned out to be sociable and accepted my invitation. To try to compensate him somehow for the trouble of posing for the photos, I offered him some milk. I put the saucer in the hallway and went back to my room to get the camera ready. I was loading a new roll of film when I heard a sharp, loud yell: 'Open up! Police!' Now, my conscience is clear, but a visit from the police is not something that's usually considered a pleasure. I was unsettled. I ran to open the door and... Can you guess who was there?"

Mr Nosegoode looked at him in suspense.

"I have no idea," he answered.

"Nobody! Nobody at all! As I was standing there, your dog slipped past my legs and ran off home. Now, can you explain to me who let out that fearsome cry? Surely it couldn't have been your dog!"

Both of them looked at Cody, who was crouching on the floor by the table as the biggest surprise of his entire life began to sink in. The criminal and poisoner turned out to be a friend of dogs! Could there be anything more astonishing? But there was no time to ponder this further because he could see a question in Ambrosius's face: tell the truth or lie?

Ambrosius didn't get a clear answer. The dog blinked at him, curled up in a ball and pretended to be asleep.

Hesitating, the detective began slowly.

"Hmm... Well, you see, Cody and I understand each other very well. So well that we even have conversations."

Blackbeard was dumbfounded.

"Conversations?"

"Yes. Maybe it really was Cody who cried out 'Police!' Maybe that's how he tried to save his life. Because he was convinced that you wanted to poison him. But I'd rather not ask him about it just now because he really doesn't like to be questioned."

Blackbeard looked wide-eyed from Ambrosius to Cody and back to Ambrosius.

"Please don't joke at my expense," he whispered.

I'm going to prove we're not joking! Cody thought.

A moment later, an indistinct mutter could be heard in the room: "Yes, it was me who cried out."

Blackbeard gaped at Cody, who hadn't even budged, and then looked back at Ambrosius. "I'm sorry, what did you say?"

Ambrosius, however, pretended not to hear and reached for the wine bottle. The guest was baffled.

"So..." He looked at Cody. "You... you can really talk?!"

Cody glanced at him with one eye, as if he wanted to say, "I can talk, I can sing, and sometimes I even play the flute... I can do all sorts of things."

A moment passed before Blackbeard could speak again. When he had got over the initial shock, he jumped out of his seat, grabbed Cody by the front paws and blurted out, "This could cause a worldwide sensation! In all of history, there has never been a case like this! You will have pride of place in my book! You're going to become the most famous dog under the sun! Because I am really hoping that you'll agree to pose for photographs and talk with me like you do with Mr Nosegoode! We'll be friends!"

Cody listened to these excited words with his usual modesty. He muttered something which could have meant, "Who knows... perhaps... perhaps..."

Meanwhile, Mr Nosegoode addressed his guest again. "I'd love to know a bit more about that bottle with a skull and crossbones which Cody told me about. He was in shock."

Blackbeard started laughing.

"That was flea poison," he explained. "I'm sorry, Cody, for being so blunt, but close contact with dogs has its unpleasant side as well. That's why I always bring that bottle with me. But how did Cody get the idea that I was a criminal? Why did he suspect I wanted to poison him?"

"It's all because of that fake beard of yours," Ambrosius replied. "Cody thought that a person who puts on a beard like that must be scheming to do something wicked."

Blackbeard jumped.

"Because of the beard?! But that completely demolishes my theory about the effect of facial hair on dogs' friendliness! For years I've been claiming that a beard

and a moustache, as relics of primeval times, make dogs less shy and inspire their trust in humans. That's why I wear this fake beard. Have I been wrong all this time?"

"No, I think it's Cody who's wrong in this instance. You said yourself that he's an exceptional dog. As such, he sometimes has different views from ordinary dogs about certain things. And that's why the beard seemed suspicious to him."

"Of course!" Blackbeard agreed. "It makes perfect sense for an exceptional dog to have unusual views.

Thank you for pointing that out. Cody has proved yet again that he's absolutely extraordinary."

Cody wagged his tail and perked up his ears. What a pleasure it was to hear such things!

Ambrosius spoke again.

"I'm guessing – no, I'm positive, that Cody will let you photograph him tomorrow. He'll agree out of great respect for the author of *Portraits of Extraordinary Dogs.*"

Blackbeard listened to these words with a slight blush, which could just about be seen through his bushy beard. He said that it would make him very happy and began saying goodbye.

"Mrs Hardtack is expecting me for dinner," he explained. "I can't be late."

After the door had closed behind him, Cody let out a groan. "Ambrosius! I'm the stupidest dog under the sun! How could I have taken this charming man for a criminal?"

Ambrosius spread his arms out wide.

"I don't understand it either."

Cody scratched his left ear vigorously, as if it were to blame.

"I really admire you," he continued. "You knew straight away that he was innocent. How could you tell?"

"I've already explained it to you. From the beard."

"But how?"

"It's simple. A criminal tries to blend in. Meanwhile, everything Blackbeard was doing made him stand out. So he couldn't be a criminal. Is that clear now?"

"Clear as the sky on a cloudless day! But only now. You know, I'm starting to wonder whether humans aren't sometimes smarter than dogs."

"An interesting question," Ambrosius acknowledged. "Let me know when you've reached your conclusion."

"It'll be my pleasure. But now that we've dealt with Blackbeard," Cody said, becoming more animated, "you finally have to tell me who stole the music box! I'm dying to know."

"I'm afraid you're going to have to wait a bit longer. You'll find out who the thief is later on, after dinner."

"After dinner?" Cody frowned, but he quickly cheered up again. "That's fine. In that case, let's go for dinner! I'd love to have a decent bone."

"I'm sorry, but we're not going to have dinner today until seven o'clock."

"What time? I must have misheard."

"Seven. But if you're hungry now, I can give you a treat. Would you like anything?"

After a brief struggle with himself, Cody replied with a superior air, "No, thank you. I've lost my appetite."

"Don't be upset." Ambrosius tried to smooth things over. "If I'm postponing dinner, I must have my reasons."

"Reasons!" Cody snorted. "You humans always manage to find a stick when you want to hit a dog. What have you thought up now?"

"I haven't thought up anything. I just don't want to have to go out twice: now for dinner and then again later in the evening."

"In the evening? Why would you go out in the evening?"

"To meet the thief."

Cody jumped.

"You're meeting the thief today?"

"Yes."

"Does the thief know?"

"No. My visit... I'm sorry – our visit – is going to be a surprise."

"You're planning to take me with you to this meeting?"

"Of course. Unless you don't want to come?"

"I do!" the dog reassured him eagerly, forgetting all about his grudge from a moment earlier.

They went out into the garden and there, in silence, pondered the adventure awaiting them. Cody curled up in a ball in a wicker armchair, wondering who this mysterious individual was whom Ambrosius believed to be the thief. Ambrosius, rocking back and forth in another armchair, contemplated the possible ways of making the thief own up to the crime.

In the meantime, the sun dipped lower and lower, growing larger and redder. When it got as low as the tops of the trees, Ambrosius stood up, stretched and announced, "Enough ruminations! I'm inviting you to the Marrow Inn for a double portion of bones!"

At the mention of bones, Cody catapulted out of his chair.

"A double portion!" he exclaimed, wagging his tail happily. "Ambrosius, you're extraordinary!"

CODY CAN'T
BELIEVE HIS EARS

They ate dinner in excellent spirits. Afterwards, Mr Nosegoode lit his pipe and Cody tried to imagine what could be more enjoyable than eating. He concluded that there was nothing better in the world.

At half past seven, the two friends left the inn and headed towards the chemist's.

Hmm, is that where we're going to find the thief? The dog was surprised. *How interesting!*

The pharmacy was closed, but a sign on the door stated that in urgent cases visitors should ring the bell to Mr and Mrs Swallowtail's private residence.

"Is our case urgent?" Cody asked when they stopped in front of the door, which was marked with a door plate that read "Z. and B. Swallowtail".

"Of course!" Ambrosius replied, examining the door plate closely.

"What's so interesting about that sign?" the dog asked.

"One very important letter," the detective replied and rang the bell.

The door was opened by Mr Swallowtail, who greeted his guests warmly and invited them in.

"We're just drinking some tea and we'd be delighted if you would join us," he said.

Indeed, the whole family was sitting at the table, with steaming cups of tea in front of them. The arrival of unexpected guests disrupted this familiar atmosphere.

Mrs Swallowtail quickly got up from the table, greeted the visitors with a rapid torrent of words and made sure that Mr Nosegoode was comfortably installed in the seat of honour. Smiling brightly, she went to get an extra teacup from the kitchen.

"How about something nice for the doggy?" she asked from the doorway, which touched Cody deeply.

Mr Nosegoode thanked her and looked around at the other members of the family. The chemist's daughter was a slim girl with a cutely turned-up nose. From the way she was looking at Cody, it wasn't hard to guess that she adored dogs. Her younger brother had the look of a future inventor. If the Chinese hadn't already invented gunpowder, it surely would have been discovered by the young Swallowtail. The last person Ambrosius's eyes rested upon was Ben. The chemist's nephew didn't return his interest. He was staring at the ceiling, as if there were far more fascinating things going on there than a visit from a detective.

Mrs Swallowtail came back and another flood of words poured out.

"Here's your tea, Inspector! How about a biscuit? I baked these myself. I'm so glad that you've decided to pay us a visit. I've heard so much about you!"

She caught her breath and asked in a whisper, "Do you have any news?"

"I do indeed, Mrs Swallowtail. I bring good news and... and your gloves."

Mrs Swallowtail's outstretched hand, which was about to pass Mr Nosegoode his tea, froze in mid-air.

"Gloves? What gloves are you talking about, Inspector?"

"These," Ambrosius replied, handing her the pair of black silk gloves which he had found that morning in the bushes.

The chemist's wife glanced at them and cried out in astonishment.

"My gloves! Where did you find them?"

"Oh, not far from here. I'm very glad I can return them to you."

Mrs Swallowtail was so surprised she didn't even ask Mr Nosegoode how he knew that the gloves belonged to her.

"Now I have no doubts at all that you're going to find the thief!" she said with deep conviction.

"I've already found the thief," Ambrosius announced.

The room went silent. Ambrosius pretended not to notice the inquisitive looks all around him and reached for his pipe as if nothing had happened. He filled it with tobacco and asked if he could smoke. He then took a box of matches out of his pocket and, without hurrying, lit the pipe and put the matchbox on the table. He did it in such a way as to ensure that one of those present could clearly see the numbers written on the box:

4.25

7.15

21.30

Inhaling deeply, he closely observed the individual in question. He could see fear in the person's eyes and noted without surprise that the thief's hand shook as it reached for the teacup...

The chemist was the first to speak.

"You said just a moment ago that you know who the thief is. Can you share the culprit's name with us?"

"Of course."

"I think we should go to see this person straight away and claim our property back," Mrs Swallowtail exclaimed.

"That won't be necessary," the detective said.

"How so?"

"It won't be necessary," he continued, "because the thief is in this room."

His words produced a staggering effect on the assembled company. Mrs Swallowtail clutched her head in disbelief. Mr Swallowtail wanted to protest, but for a few seconds he was speechless. Cody couldn't believe his ears, and he lifted his head so abruptly that he hit it on the seat of a chair. Meanwhile, the person on whom Ambrosius's eyes were resting tried to get up from the table but didn't have enough strength...

"You must be joking," the chemist finally stammered out. "That's not possible!"

"I'm not joking," the detective replied seriously. "The person who stole the music box is among us. I hope I'm not going to have to point them out with my finger. I hope this person stands up and confesses voluntarily."

Mr Nosegoode finished talking and gazed somewhere

off into the corner. A heavy silence fell in the room. Only the clock could be heard counting the passing seconds. Suddenly, a chair scraped against the floor. Everyone looked in the direction of the sound and saw... Ben standing up.

"Ben?" Mrs Swallowtail groaned.

"So it's you?" The chemist couldn't believe his eyes.

Ben hung his head low and said nothing.

"Go to your room and bring us the music box," Ambrosius said quietly.

Ben obeyed.

The atmosphere at the table was distinctly uncomfortable. Mr Swallowtail was sullen. The younger Swallowtails sat motionless with their eyes fixed firmly on their teacups. Cody was experiencing his second enormous surprise of the day. As for Mrs Swallowtail, she kept rubbing her temples and saying, "Well, I never... I would've never thought... Never!

"How did you work out that it was Ben, Inspector?" she finally asked.

Mr Nosegoode removed the pipe from his mouth, weighed it briefly in his hand and then began to speak.

"From the beginning, I assumed that the music box held some kind of secret and that it was stolen by someone who knew that secret. There were many suspects: neighbours, family, the clockmaker's apprentice... From talking to you, Mr Swallowtail, I learnt about Ben, and I immediately became suspicious. Ben went to the clockmaker's the day before the theft and asked when the music box would be ready, seemingly on your behalf. 'My uncle can hardly wait,' he said as he was leaving. I wondered why you didn't pick up the music box that same day if you were in such a hurry. There could be only one answer: Ben didn't tell you that it had been repaired. My suspicions were confirmed during our conversation. You said that Ben gave you this important news only yesterday morning. Why did he delay? It's not hard to guess. He had gone to ask after the music box because he needed to find out about it for himself. Ben wanted to get the treasure. He realized that whoever laid their hands on the repaired music box first would be the one to find the treasure. That's why he kept an eye on it and asked about it. He told you about his visit to the clockmaker's only when the music box was already in his possession.

"But these were just theories," the detective continued, "and I needed evidence. Luckily, the thief left behind a few souvenirs: a silk thread (which, as I rightly guessed,

came from a glove), a shoe print, a mark left by a crowbar and a box of matches. *If Ben really was the culprit,*
I thought to myself, *then by following in his footsteps, I*
should be able to find some traces. Perhaps the gloves, perhaps
the crowbar? I was right. In a clump of bushes halfway
between Mr Blossom's workshop and your house, I found
both the gloves and the crowbar. When I got home, I
compared the thread that the thief had left on the door
of the workshop with the gloves. There was no doubt
whatsoever that the gloves were the ones the thief had
used. And the initials embroidered on them led me to
believe that they belonged to this household.

"Another clue was provided by the box of matches. This one." Mr Nosegoode pointed to the matchbox lying in front of him. "I found out from you, Mr Swallowtail, that Ben had been planning to visit his parents yesterday. His parents live in Duckfield, don't they?" He turned to the chemist. Mr Swallowtail nodded.

"Well, the music box enthusiast was also planning a trip there. I realized this from a series of mysterious numbers which Mr Blossom's night visitor had written on the matchbox. Take a look! I soon guessed their meaning: these are train departure times. I went to the station and quickly found them on the timetable. There are trains leaving for Duckfield at exactly 4.25, 7.15 and 21.30. The evidence against Ben was mounting. Just in case, I went to ask Joey Humming, another suspect, about Duckfield. Joey's surprise was so sincere that it cleared him of all suspicion. That left Ben. Today – at this table – I subjected him to the final test. I made sure that he saw the gloves and the matches. His reactions convinced me that my suspicions had been correct. I decided to take a risk: I called on Ben to confess his guilt. And he did."

Mr Nosegoode lit his pipe, which had gone out during the course of his tale, and took a few puffs.

"What if the test hadn't gone as planned?" the chemist asked matter-of-factly. "What if Ben hadn't confessed? What would you have done? After all, my wife's gloves could have easily been stolen by someone else, and Ben isn't the only person who goes to Duckfield."

"Please don't forget that I had two other pieces of evidence up my sleeve: the shoe print and a handwriting sample on the matchbox. If Ben hadn't confessed, I would have used them."

Mrs Swallowtail couldn't contain herself any longer.

"You're a miracle worker!" she declared.

"I'm just an old detective, Mrs Swallowtail!" Ambrosius corrected her modestly.

At that moment, Ben came back holding the music box. He put it down on the table without a word.

All eyes were immediately drawn to it – this old family keepsake that was supposed to show the way to a treasure.

THE TREASURE

Silence filled the room once more. The small box, with its porcelain dancer and its mysterious secret, had them all in its power. A little key for winding the mechanism stuck out of an opening on the side. A few turns of the key and the music box would break its silence. But what would it say? Would it really show the way to the treasure? These questions were on everyone's mind.

Mr Swallowtail turned to Ben.

"Have you tried winding it yet?" he asked, pointing to the box.

Ben shook his head.

"I was afraid," he blurted out. "I was afraid that someone would hear."

"So why did you steal it?"

"I was going to take it home. I'd wind it there and come back for the treasure..."

The chemist nodded. "I should really punish you severely," he declared.

He picked up the music box and said, "Let's hear this dancing girl! It's time to find out if what my grandfather wrote is true."

The room was filled with a rasping sound as he wound up the mechanism. There was a tense pause – and then they heard the first silvery tones of a lively melody. The porcelain ballerina spun into action. They all listened intently to the tune, waiting for some hint as to where the treasure was hidden – but in vain. There was nothing to be guessed from the melody.

"So?" Mrs Swallowtail asked with disappointment in her voice.

"So nothing," her husband answered in the same tone.

Only Mr Nosegoode was of a different opinion.

"It seems to me," he said, "that the melody contains a clue..."

"What!" Mr and Mrs Swallowtail cried out together.

"It contains a clue," the detective continued. "But to decipher it you need to know the words to the song. I'm guessing you're not familiar with them?"

"This is the first time I've heard this melody," Mrs Swallowtail admitted.

"Luckily, I know this song. I remember it from my childhood. My mother would often sing it. Here's how it begins:

What's inside the fireplace
going crick-crick-crick?
Look carefully for a cricket
And you'll find it quick.

"*Inside the fireplace*," Mr Nosegoode repeated emphatically. "Does that not tell you something?"

All eyes fell on the corner of the room, where there was an elaborate antique fireplace.

"You think it's in there, Inspector?" the chemist asked.

"Yes. If the treasure exists, that's where it must be hidden."

The two of them went up to the fireplace and looked at it in silence.

"I have no idea how a treasure could be hidden in there," Mr Swallowtail said, scratching his head.

"These old fireplaces often have a secret compartment that nobody even suspects exists," Ambrosius said and looked inside. "It's so dark in here! I can't see any opening at all. I wonder how the smoke got out?"

"There was an opening once," the chemist explained, "but it's been blocked up. That was during my grandfather's time. Ever since, the fireplace has just been for decoration."

"All the better," the detective muttered and began thoroughly examining the outside of the fireplace. He knocked on one brick after another, he listened, he looked into every little nook and cranny...

He paused at one particular brick. At first glance it didn't seem any different from the others. It was just a bit larger and a shade darker and – most crucially – it made a hollower sound when struck.

When Ambrosius leant down and looked at it from below, he noticed something the others couldn't see: a small dark button that blended in well with the deep-red colour of the brick. He pressed it, and something unexpected happened. There was a grating noise and the brick rotated on its axis, revealing a dark cavity.

"A secret compartment!" Mrs Swallowtail blurted out.

"You're right!" the chemist exclaimed.

"Open Sesame," the detective said with a bow.

Mr Swallowtail understood that Mr Nosegoode was waiting for him. As the descendant and rightful heir of his grandfather, he should be the first to examine the contents of the compartment. He cast a quick glance at his wife and children and, seeing encouragement in their eyes, stepped towards the hole. He put his hand inside and rummaged around for a long time – an awfully long time, it seemed. At last, he pulled his hand back out, clutching something. It was a small metal box. He opened it easily. And inside was...

"A bottle!" He let out a stifled cry.

Indeed. The chemist took out what looked like a little medicine bottle. It had a small label on the outside, and inside was a cloudy liquid.

Mr Swallowtail set it down on top of the fireplace and reached into the compartment once again. This time he pulled out a small glass jar with a piece of paper rolled up inside it.

"That's everything," he declared, wiping his hands.

His voice betrayed neither joy nor disappointment. He said it as if he were saying, "It's raining," or "Tomorrow's Saturday."

"What's in the bottle?" his wife asked uneasily.

The chemist held the bottle up to his eyes and read out the faded inscription, syllable by syllable: "For-get-ful-ness po-tion.

"Forgetfulness potion!" he repeated in astonishment.

"Forgetfulness potion!" his son echoed.

"A potion!" his daughter exclaimed.

Everyone was stunned. Could it be that Mr Swallowtail's grandfather, well known for his mischievous nature, had decided to play another wicked joke on his family?

They all turned their eyes to the jar containing the rolled-up note. Perhaps it held the answer to this very question? Mr Swallowtail nervously removed the lid, pulled out the piece of paper, unrolled it and read out loud:

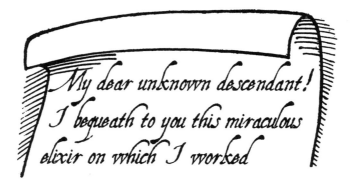

My dear unknown descendant! I bequeath to you this miraculous elixir on which I worked

for many long years. I discovered it only in the autumn of my life. It has the very special power to erase unpleasant or painful events from memory. If you carry inside you something which you would rather forget, concentrate all your thoughts on it and take three drops of this potion. Whatever has pained you like a splinter will disappear without a trace, and the cause of your distress will never again be repeated. I command you, however, to use my invention honestly and wisely.

Your forebear

Mr Swallowtail finished reading. Holding the open letter in his hands, he looked at the others. They all had expressions of disbelief painted on their faces.

Only Ben's eyes lit up with a glimmer of hope.

"I'm sure your grandfather has made fools of us all," said Mrs Swallowtail, clearly the most disappointed among them. "There's a good reason why his family thought he was an ill-tempered crackpot."

"People often label as crackpots those whom they can't understand," Mr Nosegoode replied.

"You believe in this potion?" Mrs Swallowtail asked, surprised.

"I wasn't talking about the potion. I was talking about an old man who was considered to be an eccentric by his family."

Mrs Swallowtail wanted to add something, but Ben interjected.

"Dear Uncle," he said quietly, "if you would just allow me to test this potion..."

"You'd like to try it out?"

"Yes. I don't think three drops can hurt."

The chemist was undecided. He looked at his wife and then at Mr Nosegoode.

"Well, if he wants to..." Mrs Swallowtail shrugged.

"I don't have anything against it either," the detective added.

The chemist picked up the bottle containing the miraculous potion and carefully pulled out the stopper.

"It smells nice," he remarked. He turned to Ben. "Come here with a teaspoon."

Ben grabbed a teaspoon off the table and ran up to his uncle.

"Do you know what you want to forget?" Mr Swallowtail asked him.

"Yes."

There was so much shame and remorse in that one

word that everybody instantly guessed exactly what Ben wanted to erase from his memory.

Three drops of the potion dripped down into the spoon.

"Go ahead," the chemist said solemnly.

Ben closed his eyes, concentrated for a moment and swallowed the drops. He stood motionless for a few seconds before opening his eyes and looking all around.

"And?" his uncle and aunt asked at the same time.

Ben tried to remember something, but from his helpless expression it was clear that he couldn't.

"So, have you forgotten about the theft?" Mrs Swallowtail got impatient.

"What theft?" Ben asked, perplexed.

"Don't you pretend!" his aunt warned him.

"I'm not pretending. Auntie, I really have no idea what you mean."

He sounded so sincere that Mrs Swallowtail seemed to lose her confidence. She pondered something briefly and then turned to her husband.

"Bonnie! Give me three drops! I have to see for myself."

The chemist obliged. Mrs Swallowtail swallowed the potion and ran a hand over her forehead.

"Just a minute... Just a minute... I wanted to forget about something, but what? How funny! I forgot what I wanted to forget about. What was it?... No, I can't remember..."

"So it's true!" Mr Swallowtail said and carefully put the bottle down on the fireplace.

*

Ambrosius sensed that it was time to say goodbye. He had played his role. He had unmasked the thief, recovered the music box and found the treasure. Now all that remained was to notify Mr Blossom of the successful resolution of the case – and then he could turn his attention back to his radishes.

"Please stay a while longer, Inspector!" Mr and Mrs Swallowtail pleaded when he got up from his chair. "We're in your debt! We'd like to pay you back somehow."

"A kind word is all I need," Mr Nosegoode replied with a smile. "I'm very happy I could help you."

"What about a few drops of the potion?" the chemist suggested.

"No, thank you. I want to remember everything I have lived through. Both the good and the bad."

Mr and Mrs Swallowtail were downcast.

"We'll never forget this good turn you've done us, Inspector!"

Mr Nosegoode kissed Mrs Swallowtail's hand, said his goodbyes to the other members of the family and left.

It was nearly dark outside in the street, where an elderly man was lighting the old gas lamps. The windows of houses lit up one by one as night enveloped the town.

"Ambrosius!" Cody said. "I bow my nose to you. You are the most brilliant detective and I'm the stupidest of all dogs. But is it my fault that there are more things on earth than are dreamt of by dogs?"

"You are the nicest of all dogs," Ambrosius said, rubbing Cody's back.

PUSHKIN CHILDREN'S BOOKS

We created Pushkin Children's Books to share tales from different languages and cultures with younger readers, and to open the door to the wide, colourful worlds these stories offer.

From picture books and adventure stories to fairy tales and classics, and from fifty-year-old bestsellers to current huge successes abroad, the books on the Pushkin Children's list reflect the very best stories from around the world, for our most discerning readers of all: children.